# Tell Me Again
## About the Night I Was Born

by Jamie Lee Curtis
illustrated by Laura Cornell

SCHOLASTIC CANADA LTD.

The author wishes to thank profusely
Laura Cornell, Joanna Cotler, and Phyllis Wender.

**Canadian Cataloguing in Publication Data**
Curtis, Jamie Lee, 1958-
Tell me again about the night I was born
ISBN 0-590-03839-7
I. Cornell, Laura. II. Title.
PZ7.C978Te 1998     j813'.54     C98-931293-3

8 7 6 5 4 3          Printed and bound in Canada          1 2 3 4 5 / 0

For Annie, Tom and Chris
~J.L.C.

For Lilly
~L.C.

Tell me again about the night I was born.

Tell me again how you and Daddy were curled up like spoons and Daddy was snoring.

Tell me again how the phone rang in the middle of the night and they told you I was born.
Tell me again how you screamed.

Tell me again how you called Granny and Grandpa right away, but they didn't hear the phone because they sleep like logs.

Tell me again how you got on an airplane with my baby bag and flew to get me and how there was no movie, only peanuts.

Tell me again how you held hands all the way to the hospital and when you got there you both got very quiet and felt very very small.

Tell me again about the first time you saw me through the nursery window and how you couldn't believe something so small could make you smile so big.

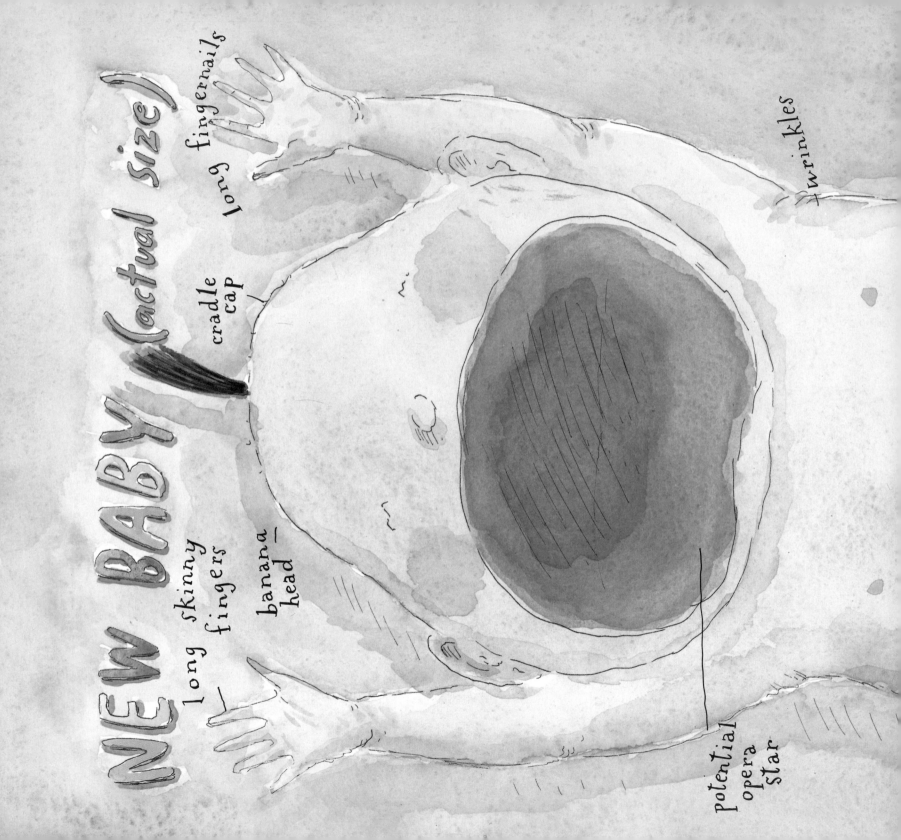

NEW BABY (actual size)

long fingernails

cradle cap

twinkles

long skinny fingers

banana head

Potential opera star

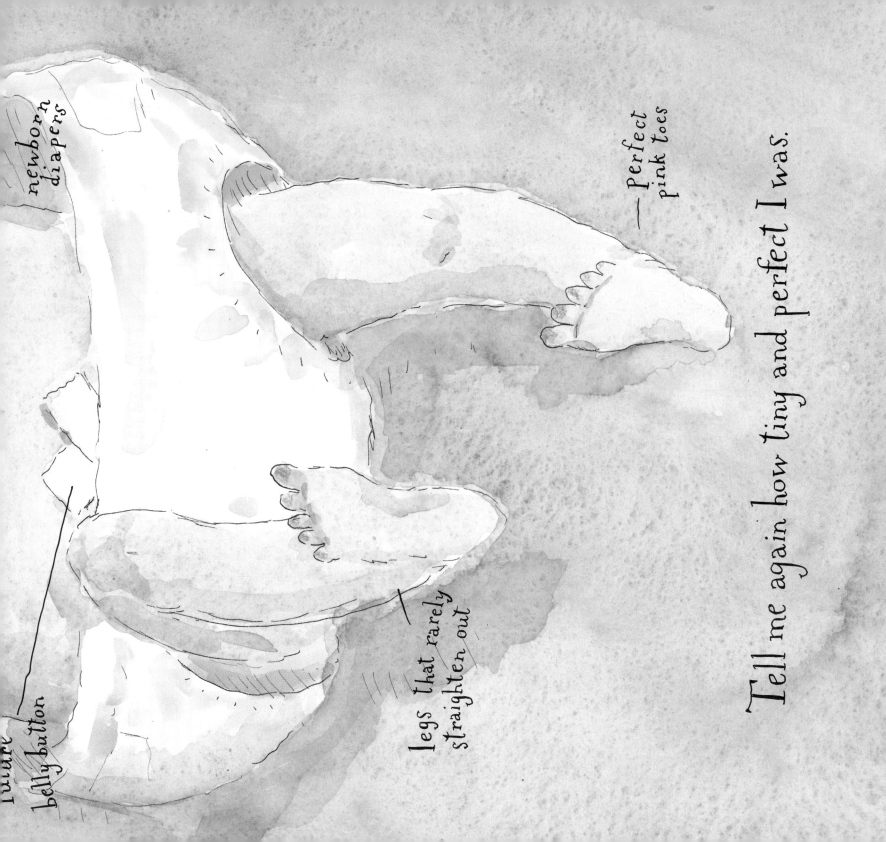

newborn
diapers

future
belly button

legs that rarely
straighten out

Perfect
pink toes

Tell me again how tiny and perfect I was.

Tell me again about the first time you held me
in your arms and called me your baby sweet.
Tell me again how you cried happy tears.

Tell me again how you carried me like a china doll all the way home and how you glared at anyone who sneezed.

Tell me again about the first night you were my daddy and you told me about baseball being the perfect game, like your daddy told you.

TUB O' LARD

Tell me again about the first night you were my mommy and you sang the lullaby your mommy sang to you.

Tell me again about our first night as a family.

Mommy, Daddy, tell me again about the night I was born.